Hey Jack! Books

The Crazy Cousins

The Scary Solo

The Winning Goal

The Robot Blues

The Worry Monsters

The New Friend

The Worst Sleepover

The Circus Lesson

The Bumpy Ride

The Top Team

The Playground Problem

The Best Party Ever

First American Edition 2013
Kane Miller, A Division of EDC Publishing

Text copyright © 2013 Sally Rippin
Illustration copyright © 2013 Stephanie Spartels
Logo and design copyright © 2013 Hardie Grant Egmont

First published in Australia in 2013 by Hardie Grant Egmont

For information contact:
Kane Miller, A Division of EDC Publishing
P.O. Box 470663
Tulsa, OK 74147-0663
www.kanemiller.com
www.edcpub.com
www.usbornebooksandmore.com

Library of Congress Control Number: 2012956113
Printed and bound in the United States of America
2 3 4 5 6 7 8 9 10
ISBN: 978-1-61067-186-6

Hey Jack!

The Circus Lesson

By Sally Rippin

Illustrated by Stephanie Spartels

Kane Miller

A DIVISION OF EDC PUBLISHING

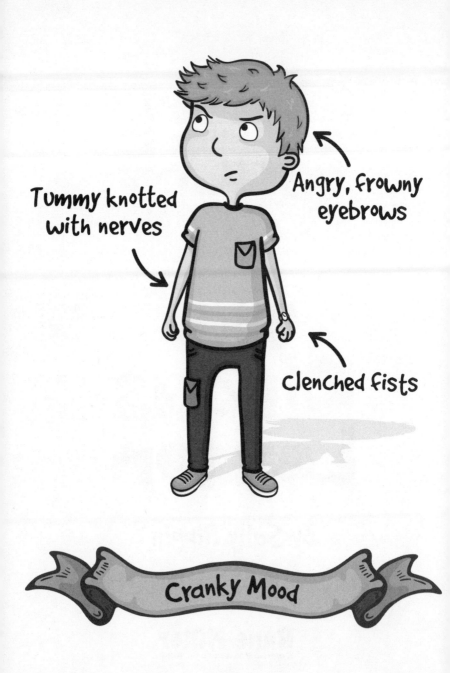

Chapter One

This is Jack.

Today Jack is in

a cranky mood.

His parents are going

away for the night.

Jack's cousin Sue is coming to take care of him. Jack doesn't *want* Sue to come.

He hasn't even met her before. He wants to go away with his mom and dad. They **always** take him away with them!

2

"You'll have fun
with Sue," says
Jack's mom.

"No, I won't!" says Jack.
"I want to come
with you."

"You can come
with us next time,"
says Jack's dad.
"This time we want to
do something different."

Jack crosses his arms

and stomps his foot.

"It's not fair!" he shouts.

4

Then he runs upstairs
and hides under
his bed. *Maybe if Mom
and Dad can't find me,
they won't go away,*
he thinks.

It is dark and
squeezy under
Jack's bed. The dust
tickles his nose.

5

Jack breathes through his mouth so he won't sneeze. *They'll be sorry when they see that I'm gone,* he thinks.

Just then, Jack's dad
pokes his head
under the bed.

"Hey, Jack," he says.
"Sue is here. Come out
and say hello."

Jack **shuffles** out
from under the bed.
He brushes the dust balls
off his tummy.

7

"Hello," he says, looking down at the ground.

"Hey, Jack," says Sue. "Nice to meet you."

"OK, it's time for us
to go," Jack's dad says.
"See you tomorrow."

"Bye, darling," Jack's
mom says. "I love you."

No, you don't, thinks Jack.
*If you loved me you
wouldn't go without me.*

Jack listens to
his parents walk
downstairs with Sue.

He hears them

talking in the kitchen.

Then he hears

the front door close.

The house is very quiet.

Jack sits on his bed

and tries not to cry.

He feels sad and

lonely and a

little bit **grumpy**.

10

Suddenly Jack hears
Scraps, his dog, barking.
And then he hears
another noise too.

It sounds like

a dog howling,

mixed with a walrus

snorting. It is

the strangest sound

he has ever heard.

Jack hops down off

the bed and creeps

down the stairs.

The sound is coming

from the family room.

Jack peers around

the doorway.

There, in the middle

of the room,

is a very odd sight!

Sue has changed

into a sparkly leotard.

She is standing on
her head and singing –
very loudly!

Chapter Two

"Oh, hi there!"

Sue shouts.

"I wasn't bothering

you, was I?"

She flips back
onto her feet
and takes out
her earphones.
"That's better," she says
in a quieter voice.
"I can't hear
how **loud** I'm talking
when I have
my earphones in."

Jack's mouth drops open.
"What are you doing?"
he asks.

"Practicing," says Sue.
"I have a show
on Monday."

"A show?" asks Jack.

"Yes," says Sue.
"I'm an acrobat
in the circus."

"Oh," says Jack.

An acrobat! He feels

a flutter of excitement.

"So … do you sing, too?"

"No, no," Sue says,
laughing loudly.
"My circus mates
would kill me!
I just like to sing
while I practice.
Sorry, I hope your
eardrums are OK."

Jack nods and giggles.

"Right!" says Sue.

She puts her hands on her hips. "So, what do you usually do at this time of night?"

"Er... have dinner?"
Jack says.

"Great!" says Sue.

"What are we having?"

Jack looks **worried**.

"Just kidding!" says Sue.

"I can cook.

But I prefer takeout,

don't you?"

"Shall we get pizza?" asks Sue. "Because it's a special occasion."

"Er... sure!" says Jack. "I guess so."

Sue jogs over to the phone. "I like mine **extra-extra** cheesy," she calls out to Jack. "Is that OK?"

"Yes!" says Jack.

"I like mine cheesy, too!"

While they wait for
the pizza to arrive,
Sue does some more
acrobatics.

23

Handstands, flips,

backbends.

She is amazing.

Jack and Scraps

watch the show.

When she's done,

Jack claps **wildly**.

Then Sue teaches

Jack how to juggle!

24

Finally, the doorbell rings.

"Pizza's here," Sue calls.
"Hooray! I'm starving."

"Shall I set the table?"
asks Jack.

"Nah," says Sue.
"Then we have to
wash our dishes.
Let's just have a
picnic on the floor."

26

Jack feels worried. "Mom doesn't like me eating in the family room," he says. "We might spill food on the carpet."

"Hmm..." says Sue, frowning. "I know! Why don't we eat outside in your playhouse?"

"Really?" says Jack.

"Sure!" says Sue. "It's good to eat outside. Everything tastes better in the fresh air."

28

So Jack and Scraps
and Sue all squeeze
into the playhouse.
They eat the pizza
with their hands,
and Scraps licks their
fingers clean.

Sue is right. It is
the **yummiest** pizza
Jack has ever eaten.

29

Chapter Three

It is getting dark.
"I should get ready
for bed," Jack says.
"It's late."

"Aw, really?" says Sue.

"But we're having
so much fun. Oh,
I know! Why don't we
sleep out on the grass?
Under the stars."

Jack gasps. "Really?

But won't we need

a tent or something?"

"Nah," says Sue.

"It's a beautiful night.

I do it all the time.

Do you have

sleeping bags? I have

some netting in my car.

That way we won't get

bitten by mosquitoes."

"But won't we need
mattresses?" Jack says.
He feels **excited** and
worried at the same time.

He has never met
a grown-up like
Sue before!

"A bit of lumpy ground
never hurt anyone,"
Sue says, grinning.

In no time at all,
Jack and Sue are
in their sleeping bags
in the backyard.

Scraps lies on
Jack's feet. Jack feels
warm and snuggly.

He gazes up at
the stars through
the mosquito netting.

"This is fun," says Jack.

"Isn't it!" says Cousin Sue.

"But I still miss Mom
and Dad a little bit,"
Jack says quietly.

"I know," says Sue gently.
She gives him a squeeze.

"They will be home soon. And it's good to do things differently now and then."

Jack nods.

"When I was a little girl, I was a lot like you," Sue says.

"What do you mean?" says Jack.

38

"I liked everything to be the same," she says. "I'd get scared if things were different."

"Then what happened?"
asks Jack.

"I joined the circus!"
Sue says. "In the circus
we move around a lot.
I had to learn
not to be **scared**
of change. Doing things
differently can be
an adventure.

Just think. If your mom
and dad had never
gone away, I wouldn't
have met you, right?"

She gives Jack a cuddle.
Jack smiles. He feels
very lucky to have
met Sue. She is the
most exciting person
he has ever known.

41

Just then Jack sees

a shooting star.

"Hey, look!" he says.

"Wow! Did you make a wish?" asks Sue.

Jack nods and grins. He used to make the same wish every time.

But tonight, for the first time, Jack makes a different wish.

This is Jack.

Jack's new babysitter isn't like other grown-ups. Pizza for dinner, juggling lessons and sleeping outside without a tent! It's almost too much for Jack to handle ...

Enjoy your Pizza

Hey Jack!

AUSTRALIA
Kane Miller
EDC PUBLISHING

P8-CRK-871

9 781610 671866